EROTICA

THE PLEASURE OF SURRENDER

"Reality doesn't impress me. I only believe in intoxication, in ecstasy, and when ordinary life shackles me, I escape, one way or another. No more walls."
Anaïs Nin, *The Diary of Anaïs Nin, Vol. 1: 1931-1934*
Nicolas Blanc
Minuet Publishing
Book 1 of the 'Erotica' Series.

NICOLAS BLANC

For a free story and information about new releases subscribe to:
Minuet Publishing[1] at:

[2]

http://minuetpublishing.wix.com/books

---

1. http://minuetpublishing.wix.com/books

2. http://minuetpublishing.wix.com/books

CHAPTER 1. THE MANSION

A single chair stood upon the stage with a spotlight on it. The stage was in the ballroom of a grand estate at midnight. Several elegantly dressed women surrounded the stage. Some wore little black dresses, black stockings, and shiny high heeled black shoes. Others wore suits and had their hair cut short with floppy fringes. They sipped on cocktails and ate canapes served by young waitresses in short frilly skirts and low cut white blouses.

In a nearby room, Candice nervously applied her make up looking into a mirror with lit light globes all around it. Another young woman, Julie did the same at a different mirror. A slow salsa ballad started down the hall and the two young women knew it was time to go onto the stage. They walked down the hallway towards the ballroom. Black lace was wrapped around their eyes.

On the way, Julie grabbed Candice's hand and gave it a small squeeze. As they entered the room, the audience clapped, the lights were dimmed and a spotlight fell upon the young women. They walked together in time with the music in stunning evening dresses with long splits which revealed thigh high stockings when they stepped up onto the stage. They danced close together with each other, around the chair, circling the stage. They barely knew each other but knew what was expected of them.

Julie moved her hands down from Candice's shoulder and arm down Candice's side so that both hands rested on Candice's pert behind covered in the blue sequins of her dress, her body swaying to the music.

"Candy, hold the back of that chair while Jules pulls the zipper of your dress down with her teeth," Olivia, the owner of the mansion commanded meeting with a small amount of applause from the gathered group.

"Do it slowly," Olivia added.

Candice held the chair with a straight back and Julie had to stand on her toes in her high heeled shoes to reach the zip. Her first attempt to grab the zip with her teeth failed.

"While you are there kiss the back of Candy's neck and her ears," Olivia said, enjoying the situation, now she had the power rather than Candice.

"Try and reach the zip again Jules," Olivia continued, lighting up a cigar and puffing upon it, stamping the ash into a small silver ashtray on the table.

This time, Julie was able to grab the zip and edge it down slowly until the glittery blue dress fell to the floor. Olivia half smiled at the sight of Candice in the expensive black lingerie that Olivia had bought her for Christmas along with the necklace of large pearls which Candice was also wearing. The music stopped.

"Jules now remove Candy's underwear with your teeth," Olivia said.

Julie leant down and grabbed the side of Candice's black lace panties with her teeth and pulled them down Candice's long legs and Candice immediately put her hand down to cover herself.

"Good girl Candy. Now play with yourself," Olivia commanded.

For a moment, Candice was filled with indecision and started to wonder if there was some other way out of this situation. Someone shuffled in their seat to break the uncomfortable silence.

Candice shyly edged her fingers down and brushed them through her pubic hair a couple of times, hoping this would placate Olivia and the gathered crowd.

"Turn that chair around and sit on the edge of it with your legs wide apart," Olivia said.

Candice hesitated again.

"Don't keep us waiting. You want to win this little competition don't you?" Olivia taunted Candice with the competition that they had agreed.

Candice grabbed the chair and turned it around to face the gathered crowd of women. She lowered her head as she spread her legs apart, showing the whole room her most private self.

The women in the crowd clapped gently to show their appreciation.

"Now stroke yourself," Olivia commanded.

Candice stroked between her legs, the spotlight bearing down upon her.

"Now put two fingers in deeply," Olivia said.

Candice obeyed the request by putting two fingers in and stroked herself, applying gentle pressure to the top vagina wall.

"Jules as Candy does this, please remove your panties and offer them to someone in the crowd," Olivia directed Julie.

Julie immediately reached up under her dress and pulled her black lingerie panties down and handed them to one of the women in the front row.

"Now offer her your vagina," Olivia said and the crowd collectively held their breath for a moment.

Julie hiked her glittering red dress up and stood next to the woman in the front row who would have been in her late fifties with grey bobbed hair. The woman stroked Julie's bottom then the inside of her thighs, enjoying the softness and intimacy of Julie's skin then stroked Julie gently between her legs.

"Ladies, which of these two women would be wettest between the legs. If you vote Candy, the young woman on the stage, please raise your hand," Olivia said to the audience while Candice continued to stroke herself. About half the audience raised their hand.

"If you vote for the lovely Jules then please raise your hand," Olivia said and the other half of the room raised their hand.

"OK well, I think these two need some more incentive to win this. Let's make this interesting. The winner will get to ride the loser for our amusement. The loser will also be our personal pet for the rest of the ight. So Jules and Candy, do your best if you want an opportunity to vin," Olivia said, Candice now stroking herself with more earnest effort.

The woman from the audience also did not want to let Julie down nd stroked Julie as skillfully as she could until her fingers glistened.

"Now do we have a volunteer from the audience to be the umpire?" questioned Olivia.

A number of hands went up.

"You, Penny - you may be the umpire," Olivia pointed to a tall woman named Penelope who walked up onto the stage and leant down to judge the state of wetness of Candice by caressing her between the legs.

"I'd give her a seven on the arousal scale," Penelope said.

Penelope then went to where Julie was holding her dress up and caressed her between the legs.

"Definitely wetter. A nine," Penelope declared.

The audience applauded.

How did I get here? Candice asked herself.

CHAPTER 2. THE PITCH

The advertising office was in a whirl of activity. Candice Hughes rehearsed her presentation to the client manager and the manager of the creative team at Aspire Advertising. Candice's concept was to make the change the way the public perceived Harrison Savings and Loan with a complete makeover by using wild forests in their advertising and changing their brand to a stag with long antlers with Harrison in the middle. Candice had arranged for a video team to take some video footage and stills from the Catskill Mountains which she was using in the presentation.

"That's amazing Candice," the client manager said at the end of the presentation.

"I loved it too, Candice," said the creative team manager, "Fresh and modern. Makes banking seem wholesome."

"Let's hope the client likes it," said Candice before going to the kitchen and making sure everything was ready to serve tea and coffee.

Olivia Harrison arrived with a large entourage at the Aspire office. She was tall and sleek like a skyscraper and her presence filled the room.

Olivia's handshake was formidable and she had a deep and hearty laugh when Candice made a small joke during the presentation about bears and what they do in the woods.

Olivia enjoyed the presentation but enjoyed the presenter even more. Olivia's eyes followed every nuance of Candice's movement, the wave of her fingers, her breasts moving against her soft blouse, and the delicious curve of her tight skirt and her long legs with white high heels.

"I'm impressed," said Olivia, "But I want to talk about the details with Ms. Hughes here. Come with me to lunch at Andre's. My shout."

"I'd be delighted Ms. Harrison," Candice smiled.

"Call me Olivia," Olivia said her eyes aflame, "and if we become friends you can call me Olly."

"Thank you, Olivia," Candice replied.

Andre's was a sleek downtown French eatery with waiters in black and a menu that did not have prices on it. Just as well Olivia was paying, thought Candice.

"Now tell me about where you got the ideas for the rebranding and new advertising campaign from?" Olivia said then sipped on her red wine.

"I'm from Idaho originally. I see your primary business is home loans. I free-associated on home and thought of my own home back in Idaho which made me think of the forest which is kinda our spiritual home," Candice said.

"You must take me there some day," Olivia said.

"Where do you come from?" Candice asked.

"I'm a child of the world I'm afraid. Born in New York, educated in Switzerland. University in Oxford."

"Wow that's impressive," Candice smiled and touched Olivia's hand.

Olivia looked into Candice's eyes and smiled. Candice thought there was almost something electric in her eyes. Then she felt a hand on her leg under the table, stroking it very gently.

Clients had come on to Candice before but she had never been interested in them and besides that she was married. Somehow with Olivia things were different. Candice kept smiling as Olivia continued to stroke her leg.

"More wine, madame?" the waiter asked.

"Yes. Thank you," Olivia said without taking her eyes off Candice.

"And you, madame?"

"Yes. Thank you," Candice also did not take her eyes off Olivia and Olivia's hand stroked further up her leg. The long white table cloth covered Olivia's stroking.

Olivia took a sip of wine.

"That is divine. Try some," Olivia said holding her glass out to Candice who sipped the wine, a drop fell from her mouth onto her chin.

Olivia wiped the drip on Candice's chin with her thumb and then put her thumb to her mouth and sucked on it briefly.

"Mm. Divine," Olivia said.

Candice looked around the room but no one was watching them. Olivia's hand brushed her upper thigh very gently without taking her eyes off Candice, who brushed her hair to one side then looked back at Olivia and wondered what it would be like to kiss a woman on the lips.

"Where do you live in the city?" Candice asked.

"I live just around the corner in a penthouse overlooking Central Park. It has a beautiful view. You should come and have a look. I also have a place in the Hampdens, left to me by my father. A huge big house that has been in the family for generations. Do you have time to visit the penthouse?" Olivia asked.

"Well, only a short time. They will be expecting me back in the office fairly soon," Candice smiled.

"They can wait. It's my dime," Candice laughed.

Even though it was only a couple of blocks away, Olivia's chauffeur drove them to the apartment building. The limousine was long and shiny black with a separate compartment for the passengers. There was a small phone for Olivia to talk to her driver. He drove into a driveway on the side of the apartment building which led to basement parking.

Candice thought the view truly was magnificent and had not really truly appreciated the scale of Central Park, like a green lake surrounded by skyscraper cliffs. Olivia pointed out her favorite spot in Central Park, a shady area with a statute where there was a rose garden which included a rose named after her family.

Olivia asked her servants to take the afternoon off and put on some Miles Davis which wafted through the penthouse through some unseen speakers.

Olivia brought out two glasses of wine and a bottle and placed it on a table and sat down on a chair on the balcony, admiring the curve of Candice's behind as she stood looking out into the park.

Candice turned around to meet Olivia's gaze. There was something so deliciously taboo about being here thought, Candice. She had always fanaticized about what it would be like to be with a woman, someone who knows just how she wanted to be touched and what would make her orgasm. She sometimes came across a woman and wondered what it would be like to kiss her and how soft her lips would be.

Olivia stood up and walked to where Candice was standing and kissed her gently on the lips and was relieved to find Candice reciprocated and was welcoming to her approach. Olivia wrapped her arms around Candice and held her close, appreciating Candice's flowery perfume, the softness of her body and her hot breath upon Olivia as she kissed along the side of her face and along her ears.

Olivia held Candice's hand and led her inside to Olivia's bedroom. They sat on the edge of the bed and kissed each other on the lips. Olivia curled her hand around Candice's neck and held her close while caressing Candice's breast with her other hand over her soft blouse, feeling her nipple swell with her touch. Olivia gently leaned over with Candice onto the bed, kissing her along the neck then pulling her blouse up and kissing her along the stomach.

"I love your bra," Olivia said between kisses, "Very sexy."

Candice had her eyes closed torn between her building desire and the thought of her husband at home in their apartment. She then felt her skirt be lifted up then Olivia kissed and sucked along her legs and around her panties then peeled them down along Candice's legs and over her heels. Olivia then spread Candice's legs very wide and sucked upon her clitoris until Candice was lost in pleasure.

When Candice returned to her apartment her husband, Aaron was reading the paper at their kitchen table while the television buzzed in the background. As she entered he looked up from the paper and smiled and that look made her swell with guilt. Aaron was a genuinely decent guy who was having a break from the high-pressure world of mergers and acquisitions.

Candice tried to act normal and stroked Aaron's hair and said: "How did the writing go today Mr. A?"

"Not bad. Got lots of good ideas when I went cycling."

"Just as long as you don't write about me I'll be happy."

"All my books are about you. You know that. " Aaron joked.

•

CHAPTER 3. THE GREEN BENCH

The following day red roses arrived at Candice's office with a card simply inscribed with the initial "O" and a message "Meet by the spot at Central Park lake at three?" Candice hid the card from her co-workers who assumed the roses were from her husband and that it must be her birthday. Her close friends in the office knew that Aaron was broke and wondered who had sent her the flowers.

All day Candice wondered whether she would accept the invitation or not. In the end, she made an excuse before three and caught a cab to Central Park and hurried to the part of the park that Olivia had identified as her favorite when they were looking out from her balcony.

Candice arrived right on 3 and was disappointed to not find Olivia there. She was just thinking that she had the wrong part of the park when her mobile started to call.

"Candice?"

"Yes," answered Candice.

"You look beautiful today."

"Where are you? Can you see me?" Candice queried.

"I'm sorry baby. I got held up,"

"No problem," Candice said but did not mean it. She thought - why invite someone and not show up?

"I'll make it up to you. I'll have my driver meet you there. Hold on," Olivia said, "While we wait, can you do something for me, baby?"

"What is it?" Candice asked warily.

"When no one is looking unbutton the first two buttons of your blouse."

"What?" Candice looked around, "Where are you?"

"I'm right there with you," Olivia said, "On the phone."

Candice stuck a finger up in the air.

"I saw that," Olivia said, "Don't be rude."

"Are you spying on me?" Candice asked.

"A little," Olivia whispered, "Now unbutton those buttons."

Candice checked to see that no one was watching and unbuttone the first two buttons of her flowery blouse, revealing a small amount o cleavage.

"Devine," Olivia whispered.

"Where are you? Are you behind a tree?" said Candice lookin; around.

"Not behind a tree," Olivia giggled.

Candice looked up, "Do you have one of those drone things?"

"No. Not my style, baby," Olivia purred, "See that bench behind you. The green one. Go sit on the bench."

"OK. What are you up to?" Candice said sitting on the bench.

"Nothing," Olivia lied. She was enjoying this game.

"Now after that jogger goes by, remove your bra," Olivia whispered into the phone as a sweaty middle aged man jogged by.

"What?" Candice asked.

"Do it now and put the bra into your handbag. There's no one around you now."

Candice looked up at the apartment building where Olivia had her penthouse and suddenly worked out where Olivia was, peering down at Candice with a telescope.

Candice smiled and licked her lips, "And how is the weather up there?"

"Up where?" Olivia replied.

"Up in the clouds," answered Candice, quickly unhooking her bra and bundling it into her handbag before anyone could see. The outline of her breasts was soft and shapely underneath the soft blouse, her nipples slightly lifted against the fabric.

"The view is amazing," Olivia commented, "Blow me a kiss."

Candice puckered her lips and moved her hand to her mouth to blow Olivia a kiss in the direction of her penthouse.

"Can you stroke your breasts for me, baby?" Olivia whispered.

Candice checked in either direction and then gently stroked along the side of her breasts then against her nipples so that they were even more pronounced against her blouse.

A couple walked by hand in hand and Candice quickly moved her hands away from her breasts and frowned slightly.

"Don't worry about them, baby. Worry about me. I'm touching myself and I'm starting to get there. Don't leave me this way," Olivia almost pleaded.

"What is it that you want?" Candice whispered.

"I want you, baby. Only you," Olivia whispered back as her fingers reached down between her legs and she stroked herself while keeping the telescope trained on Candice.

"You know I'm married don't you?" Candice said.

"Don't kill the mood, baby. Your wedding ring is a bit of a giveaway. We are just playing, baby. No harm, no foul."

"When is your driver going to be here?" Candice asked.

"Well before he arrives, you need to be ready," Olivia replied.

"Ready for what?" Candice whispered as a group of businessmen in sharp suits walked by, admiring the pretty, young woman on the bench next to them with beautiful breasts.

"Ready for me of course," Olivia replied, moving her fingers deeper in a steady rhythm.

"What do you want me to do?" Candice asked.

"Baby, I can see the entire area. The coast is clear. Slip off those panties and put them in your handbag as well," Olivia said slightly breathlessly.

Candice stopped for a moment. This is madness she thought but there was some strange compulsion taking over her, a delicious pleasure in doing something completely taboo. She quickly looked from side to side and behind her. There was no one around. Candice quickly stood up and reached under her skirt and pulled down her panties and slipped them into her bag then crossed her legs.

Olivia felt red hot with arousal, "You were too quick."

"What?" asked Candice.

"I did not see your beautiful vagina," Olivia replied.

"Well, I'm afraid I can't just stand around flashing myself. Do you want me to be arrested?" Candice whispered.

"Just for five seconds. Please, baby. I'm close."

"You are very demanding," Candice replied before looking around again then when she was sure no one was about, pulled up the dress so her bare bottom was on the cold metal of the bench with her legs together. Candice stared in the direction of the penthouse.

"That is amazing," Olivia purred, "But it is hard for me to see. Could you just spread your legs a little apart?"

"I don't know," Candice replied looking around again then edged her legs a small distance apart, feeling the slight breeze below.

"That's just perfect baby. Very hot. I'm wet for you baby," Olivia whispered down the line, "Just stroke it, a little bit."

Candice checked the area then quickly rubbed herself for a few strokes before pulling her dress back over to cover herself. She could hear footsteps on the gravel behind her.

It was Olivia's driver, "Excuse me, Ms. Hughes. My employer has asked that I collect you and take you back to her penthouse for an appointment."

"Yes, of course," Candice said, walking behind the dark-suited driver, her body swaying on the gravel path.

CHAPTER 4. INTO MY ARMS

The driver did not say anything as they walked along the gravel path in Central Park. Olivia continued to talk to Candice on the telephone. Candice could tell that Olivia was getting more and more aroused.

Candice sat at the back of the limousine.

"I'm in," said Candice.

"OK, baby. Make yourself nice and hot for me. Lick your fingers and rub yourself," Olivia said.

Candice watched the crowded New York streets for a moment before turning her head away from the crowds and licked her fingers with a flick of her tongue then turned to the crowds again who were all oblivious to her.

Candice found that she was already moist as she gently stroked herself in the backseat of the limousine.

"Pay special attention to your clit," Olivia said "But, don't cum just yet. Remember I said I would make all this up to you."

"This better be special," Candice joked, her fingers becoming wetter.

When they arrived at the basement of Olivia's apartment building, the driver unlocked the level for Olivia's penthouse but waited in the basement.

"You have a good day, ma'am," the driver said as Candice disappeared into the lift.

When the door opened Olivia was wearing a coat and black stockings. Olivia leapt into Candice's arms, squeezing Candice to her.

Candice could feel something solid pressing against her belly. She snaked her hand between them to try and work out what it was. She followed the object down and it went all the way to Olivia's vagina. She separated from Olivia and pulled her coat open.

Olivia was dressed in high black stilettos, black stockings with garter belts, no bra, and no panties and had a strap on dildo which was inserted into her at one end and the other end was rising up high towards Olivia.

The sight was so strange it took Candice a little while to process what her eyes were telling her.

"So this is the surprise?" Candice said.

"It is," Olivia said, "Are you ready for me?"

"Well not for a thing of that size," giggled Candice.

"May I help?" Olivia asked.

"You may," giggled Candice again.

Olivia held Candice's hand as they walked into the lounge room.

"Candice could you please bend over that leather sofa over there," Olivia whispered into Candice's ear.

Candice let go of Olivia's hand and gingerly leaned over the leather sofa as instructed.

"Pull up your dress," Olivia requested, enjoying the site of the young advertising executive bent over the sofa.

Candice pulled up her dress revealing the two perfectly formed cheeks of her bottom and the pinkish skin between her legs.

Olivia stood back and admired Candice's bottom in detail then moved her hand back and slapped her bottom.

"Ouch. What was that?" Candice asked.

"I'm sorry. I could not resist," Olivia replied with a slight smirk.

Olivia noticed the slight red hand print upon Candice's white buttock. She kissed around the edges of the red mark.

"Can I make it better?" Olivia asked between kissing Candice's bottom and then rubbing Candice gently between the legs from behind until Candice let out a soft moan.

Olivia then crouched down and started to lick Candice between the legs and sucking on her clit. When Candice was ready Olivia stood up and eased the dildo slightly into Candice's vagina from behind, rocking gently back and forward to continue to stimulate her clit, then slowly moving forward until Olivia was thrusting deeply into Candice and stroking her breasts from behind, squeezing and pinching her nipples until she was panting.

The movement of the dildo into Candice was also causing the movement of the other end of the dildo into Olivia. Both women moved together, tingling with pleasure, lost in the moment. Candice turned around to kiss Olivia who after enjoying the long wet kiss, brought another smack down upon Candice's buttock.

"Work it harder, baby," Olivia whispered causing Candice to put more effort into moving with Olivia, causing the dildo to penetrate her even more deeply. Olivia held onto Candice's breasts strongly as if she was riding a wild animal until Candice muffled a gasp into her arm as she came.

"I thought I told you not to cum," Olivia said, either jokingly or in an annoyed way, Candice could not tell either way.

Candice did not reply but slumped over the sofa, exhausted.

"You can't cum until I cum," Olivia said, sounding like the spoilt daughter of a billionaire that she was.

Olivia walked over to a lounge chair and sat down, the obscene looking dildo still pointing skywards.

"Crawl over here," Olivia commanded.

Candice thought Olivia must be joking but when she looked over to Olivia she could tell that she was serious, all softness seemed to have drained from her.

"Don't make me wait," Olivia said harshly.

Candice got down from the leather sofa onto the thick carpeted floor, it was soft beneath her. She started to crawl, her dress bunched up around her waist, her bottom swaying seductively, her head bowed.

When Candice reached Olivia she looked up and Olivia's beautiful blue eyes were penetratingly clear as if she could see straight into Candice's thoughts. Candice could smell Olivia's musky scent.

"Suck it," Olivia commanded.

Olivia looked up at Olivia as she moved her mouth onto the obscene plastic dildo which was much larger than any man's penis she had ever come across.

Candice managed to stretch her mouth over the tip of the dild and move it up and down with her mouth, gently stimulating Olivi but for Olivia power was the main stimulant. Olivia enjoyed Candic submissively sucking the dildo in her work clothes, her hair slightl dishevelled, looking up at her with large brown eyes, dedicated to he trusting her.

"Play with yourself while you suck," commanded Olivia.

Candice followed the instruction and moved two fingers in forward movement between her legs while sucking the dildo, dribbl from her mouth lubricating her moving fingers.

"Now get on top," Olivia waived Candice forward and Candice lowered herself upon the dildo until it was deep into her and gently bounced up and down upon it, which also caused the dildo to penetrate Olivia more deeply.

"Kiss me, baby," Olivia said.

They kissed deeply, Candice's mouth was warm and wet and the beauty of the kiss caused Olivia to dive into a deep pool of pleasure where everything else faded into the background.

•

CHAPTER 5. THE NEW JOB

Aaron enjoyed his life as a writer but the truth was it was not paying the bills. His friends who he went cycling with during the day were all slowly going back to work as the economy improved. Aaron was also finding that even though he had much more time to write than before, the engine room for his ideas and dialogue was being out in the world of work. His greatest concern though was that his beautiful wife, Candice was losing respect for him. She had not said anything but it did not seem fair for her to be carrying the whole financial load of paying the bills.

Aaron signed up at an employment agency and was very surprised when the very next day he received an email advising that he had a job interview with Harrison Savings and Loan. The job was not quite his usual field but the pay and hours were very good, seeing he had been out of work for over 12 months.

Aaron arrived at the plush offices of Harrison and was ushered straight up to meet the CEO, Olivia Harrison. They shook hands and got straight down to business.

"At Harrison, we pride ourselves on only having the best people work for us. We are absolutely loyal to our employees and they are absolutely loyal to us," Olivia said.

"It's a two-way street," Aaron added, flashing his movie star smile.

"Correct," Olivia said, "And because we are dealing with people's financial affairs we need absolute respect for privacy and confidentiality."

Aaron looked at Olivia and tried to figure out where she was leading. His smile was starting to strain.

"Yes," he said.

"Can you assure me that it you work for us, you will not discuss your work, who you work for or even that you are working for with anyone? Not even your wife?" Olivia inquired.

"Absolutely," Aaron said, not quite sure why this was being demanded of him.

"Welcome aboard," Olivia shook his hand again and then introduced him to the head of legal, Tom Halbert, who had an office down the hall.

After Olivia had left, Aaron started to chat with Tom who introduced him to the rest of the department.

"Wife?" inquired Tom.

"Yes – Candice," replied Aaron.

"Kids?"

"No, not as yet," Aaron replied.

"I'm divorced myself," said Tom, "She's now living in North Carolina with a new fella. My boys call him Dad."

"That's hard," empathised Aaron.

"Yes, hardly get to see them."

"Tell me, Tom - is Ms. Henderson married?"

"No. Quite a few men have tried to get her to settle down – and some women but she's only in love with herself – and don't say that I said that," Tom said quietly.

"She's quite a looker," Aaron said.

"She's the evil Queen in Sleeping Beauty. Watch out," whispered Tom.

"I'm a big boy and I'm married so don't worry," Aaron whispered back.

Just then Olivia walked down the hallway, the staff subtly looking up to watch her stride by in her high heels, dark patterned stockings and deep blue dress with a split on the side. Aaron loved the sound of Olivia's heels as they click-clacked down the hallway.

•

CHAPTER 6. THE ART OF BECOMING

At night Olivia was feeling lonely and dialled the landline of the Hughes residence, not sure as to who would pick up the telephone.

"Hello?" said Candice into the line.

"Hello, baby," whispered Olivia.

Candice walked into her bedroom away from where Aaron and their friends were celebrating his new job.

"Olivia, how are you?" Candice said quietly into the phone while sitting on the bed.

"I can hardly hear you. Can you speak up?" Olivia laughed.

"Sorry Olivia. My husband is in the other room. We have some friends over."

"No problem. I won't be long. I was just feeling a bit horny and wanted to hear your voice," Olivia said.

"Sure. I'll call you at work tomorrow," Candice replied.

"It can't wait, baby. I need you now," Olivia was insistent.

"Olivia, I can't see you now. We have friends over," Candice repeated.

"Can't you tell them to leave?"

"No."

"OK then. Well, we'll just have to make love over the phone," Olivia said.

"Are you crazy? The people are just in the other room," Candice said.

"Can you lock the door?"

"No."

"Just one minute and then I'll leave you alone," Olivia said.

"One minute," Candice said propping a chair against the bedroom door handle.

"What are you wearing, baby?" said Olivia seductively.

"An apron over some jeans," Candice said honestly.

"Well slip those jeans down, baby. Do it fast," Olivia whispered.

"OK. OK," Candice replied, kicking off her sneakers then pulling down the jeans, leaving her in lime green panties, her apron, and blouse.

"Now the panties," Olivia continued.

Candice pulled the panties down her long legs and tossed them to where her jeans were.

"Candice?" Aaron called from the other room.

Candice covered the mouthpiece of the phone and yelled, "Just a minute."

"The apron and blouse too," Olivia continued, "And the bra."

Candice did not know why but she felt compelled to follow Olivia's suggestions until she was completely nude.

"Do you have a vibrator?" Olivia inquired.

"Yes, why?" Candice whispered.

"You know why, baby. Get it out for me. I want to hear it purr," Olivia said, stroking her breasts through her silk nightgown, pulling on her nipples.

"They'll hear it," Candice protested.

"No, they won't. Put on some music."

Candice turned the radio on. It was the top 40 countdown.

"Not quite my taste but it will do," Olivia said, "OK, let me hear it."

Candice went to her underwear drawer and pulled her small silver vibrator out, switched it on and held it up to the mouthpiece. It whirred quietly.

"Very nice," Olivia said as she stroked her legs, "Now where does it go?"

"In here," Candice said, edging the vibrator in.

"Now lie back on the bed with your legs wide apart facing the door and imagine me sucking on that beautiful clit of yours," Olivia whispered into the mouthpiece, stroking her own clit gently.

"Mhm," Candice murmured into the phone.

"Are you wet?" Olivia inquired.

"Yes," Candice said quietly.

"Well, I want you wetter. Dripping," Olivia replied.

"Candice. Can I have a hand out here?" Aaron said from the kitchen. Their friends were starting to ask after Candice.

"I have to go," Candice moaned.

"Not quite yet," Olivia whispered, "Who is the boss?"

"You are Olivia," Candice replied.

"Who owns your pussy?" Olivia asked.

"You do Olivia," Candice compliantly said, not believing her own words.

"OK now put that apron back on," Olivia demanded.

"Why?" Candice asked.

"Just do it," Olivia said more forcefully.

Candice picked up the apron from the pile of clothes and put it over her head.

"Now go and serve your guests," said Olivia and then disconnected the call.

•

CHAPTER 7. THE GAME IS ON

Aaron was enjoying his new job. It was good to have money in the wallet again. Aaron found the new work environment had provided creative fuel for his writing and had completed two chapters of his new book in one night. More than he had written than in two weeks when he was the house husband.

Candice seemed happier. She had been promoted at work after landing a big new client for the firm. Their sex had been electric since he had started back at work.

Aaron wondered whether the reason men did anything was just to get laid. He could not help but think about sex all the time. Even though they were sex much more frequently, he just wanted it more and more. He wondered whether he may be a sex addict.

Even his new boss turned him on. He loved her high heeled shoes and black stockings and the way her body swayed as she walked past his desk and the trail of her musky perfume.

One day at work Tom invited him to visit the local girlie bar at lunch. Aaron was reluctant but Tom suggested it would be fun and Aaron eventually conceded even though he felt a strong sense of guilt. They drank shooters at the bar while gorgeous women danced erotically to high energy dance or rock music. Beautiful, scantily clad waitresses walked by with drinks orders. By the end of lunch, Aaron was quite drunk and more than a little aroused. They were noisier than usual back in the office and people could tell they were tipsy and laughed quietly at them.

Jill, Olivia's secretary, approached Aaron and said, "Aaron, the boss wants to see you in her office. She said it was urgent. She could not find you earlier."

"Sure, no worries sweetheart," Aaron said then kicked himself for saying sweetheart. It was such a sexist and unprofessional thing to say. Must get a grip, he thought to himself.

Olivia was looking out her window when Aaron entered the office.

"And where have you been?"

"Sorry, one of the others just invited me out to lunch," Aaron replied.

"There's been a development," Olivia said mysteriously.

"Yes?" Aaron replied.

"Rosen Bank wants to buy us out," Olivia said still looking out the window, "I saw on your CV that you were in mergers and acquisitions previously and I need your help in trying to resist the takeover."

"Sure Ms. Harrison. I'd be more than happy to help," Aaron said, his mind starting to clear with his new responsibility.

Olivia walked up so she was straight in front of Aaron, slightly invading his personal space, looked into his eyes then said: "What do you recommend?"

"Well there's the "poison pill" defence," Aaron said looking into Olivia's eyes. They were the most amazing blue colour.

"Yes?" said Olivia, unzipping Aaron's trousers.

"Um, and there's the "staggered board" defence," continued Aaron.

"Continue," requested Olivia reaching her hand into Aaron's trousers and cupping his balls.

"Ah... and the "crown jewel" defence," Aaron said, embarrassed by the strong erection now protruding from his trousers.

"I'm listening," Olivia said harshly while stroking Aaron.

"And the "white knight." They can all be effective... depending on the... approach of the... takeover company."

Olivia had started to suck his penis, her head bobbing up and down below him, her high heeled black shoes pointing out as she knelt upon the floor. When Aaron was on the verge of coming Olivia stopped and Aaron's erection was throbbing.

"And what approach would be best for us?" Olivia said, continuing the conversation and not missing a beat.

Aaron was not sure what to do with his penis which suddenly felt like the elephant in the room.

"I would need to do ..." Aaron said as he started to cover himself up.

"And what do you think you're doing?" Olivia said harshly.

"Sorry...I..."

"Stroke it for me," Olivia requested.

"I..."

"Don't keep me waiting," Olivia said more forcefully.

Aaron gingerly stroked his penis. He had never masturbated in front of someone before.

Olivia went and sat at her desk and checked her emails.

"Don't stop," she said glancing over to the young suited man.

Jill, the secretary came in with some mail. She stared at Aaron as she walked across the room but did not say a word. She had seen stranger things in Olivia's office. Jill was quite impressed at the size of Aaron's penis. Aaron bowed his head in shame and stopped stroking. He could not believe this. What would Candice think?

"Ah, hem," Olivia said and Aaron resumed stroking his penis. Jill continued to stare at him as she left the room. She would not talk to the other staff about this. No need to spread office gossip, she thought. She would just store this for a rainy day. He might be going places, she thought.

When Olivia had finished checking her emails she walked up to Aaron again and inspected his penis up close. She could see the veins on the side of his penis and grabbed his balls again and squeezed gently.

"Who do these belong to?" she asked looking into Aaron's eyes.

Aaron could feel Olivia's hot breath upon his cheek. He leaned over to kiss her.

"Ah ah," Olivia said, putting a wagging finger between Aaron and her face while with her other hand she took over stroking Aaron's penis.

Again Olivia stared into Aaron's eyes with a penetrating stare.

"Who do these belong to?" she asked again.

"You, Ms. Harrison," Aaron said on the verge of coming.

Olivia then stopped stroking Aaron's penis and said, "Get out of my sight."

CHAPTER 8. CANDICE'S THEME

Driving home from work, Aaron felt wracked by guilt. He had never been unfaithful to Candice before. He rehearsed telling Candice what had happened at work but could not make the words sound right in his head and all of the scenarios he imagined ended with Candice storming out of their apartment and moving back in with her parents. Aaron was not really sure in his own mind what had really happened. He stopped at the florist to buy pink roses, the same type of roses Candice had in her wedding bouquet and also bought her an expensive box of Belgian chocolates.

Aaron beat Candice home from work, cooked dinner and when she entered the door placed a soft kiss on her lips, gave her the flowers and chocolate. After they finished the dinner, Aaron played a beautiful melody on his guitar which he had composed which he said was called "Candice's theme".

Candice smiled at Aaron at the end of the music and stroked the side of his cheek very gently with tears welling in her eyes.

"Aaron I need to tell you something," Candice said.

"Yes, beautiful?" Aaron replied.

"I've been seeing a client," Candice said as she looked away.

"What do you mean?"

"Seeing, you know. Romantically," Candice could not bring herself to look into Aaron's eyes.

"Who is it?" Aaron said.

"I can't say," Candice replied.

"Why not?"

"The client is high profile. Important to the company. I don't know what came over me," Candice replied.

"More important than us?" Aaron looked crushed.

"It is nothing to do with us. I still love you. You're the most beautiful, loving man I have ever met," Candice replied.

"It was just sex. I feel nothing for this person."

"I have a confession as well," Aaron said searching out Candice's eyes.

"Yes?" Candice said warily.

"Something happened at work today with one of the people at work,"

"Yes?" Candice said again.

"Again it was nothing. I had some drinks at lunch with Tom. I was a bit tipsy. There was a bit of err... sexual touching."

Candice was quiet for a moment and then said, "Well I'm glad we can be honest with each other."

Even though Candice said this Aaron could feel an icy breeze pass between them and they slept that nice facing away from each other. Aaron kept repeating "Candice's Theme" in his mind until he fell asleep. Candice kept staring at the radio alarm clock, watching the seconds tick over.

CHAPTER 9. AURELIA

In the following weeks, Candice felt like Olivia somehow knew that there was something up in her relationship with Aaron and had decided to leave her alone to allow the relationship to rebuild. The truth was that Olivia's ex-girlfriend, Aurelia, had re-entered her life and moved back in with her.

Aurelia was a dazzling Latin beauty, slender, long legged with beautiful, firm, breasts capped with rose-petal-soft areolas which Olivia was obsessed with. Olivia bought Aurelia lingerie which exposed Aurelia's nipples and asked her to wear soft silky blouses so Olivia could always see the buds of Aurelia's nipples. When they were alone in a lift together, Olivia would caress Aurelia's nipples and so they swelled against the fabric of her blouse.

Aurelia liked Olivia but sometimes found her too intense and controlling. Olivia was very much "the only child" who found it hard to share her toys when someone came over to play. Olivia always wanted to be the boss and this is what caused Aurelia to break up with her in the first place. The truth was that Aurelia needed a place to crash for a period after breaking up with another girlfriend who had admitted she was having an affair with someone else.

At least, you knew where you stood with Olivia and did not expect loyalty from her. Aurelia was surprised how quickly they went back to their old habits and how quickly the passion was inflamed again.

Olivia often requested that she watch Aurelia masturbate wearing elaborately patterned black stockings, garter belts, black bras with the nipples exposed, and high heeled patent black leather stilettos. No panties were allowed while in the penthouse. Olivia wanted free access to Aurelia whenever she wanted to touch her. Olivia also insisted that Aurelia is completely shaven so that she could see the delicate folds of Aurelia's labia.

Olivia would place a cushion on the table in front of her favourite leather chair and ask Aurelia to position herself on that cushion with her legs apart. Aurelia would caress and stroke herself for long periods of time. Olivia never tired of watching this and enjoyed watching Aurelia bring herself to orgasm, the beautiful agony of the moment or first orgasm, the build to a second orgasm, the soft moaning. Sometimes Aurelia would even cum a third time. Olivia would slowly approach Aurelia and kiss her on the lips or the genitals very softly.

Olivia would then enjoy seeing Aurelia walk around the house with no panties in her high heels in her post-orgasm state. Olivia would slip her fingers between Aurelia's legs and enjoy the warmth and wetness there.

One evening Olivia told Aurelia how she had a shy friend named Candice who had always wanted to have sex with two other women but was too shy to make that fantasy a reality. They discussed ways of making the fantasy happen for the friend and discussed how the best approach was to blindfold the friend so she could enjoy the sensuality of the experience while not being overwhelmed by the experience.

•

CHAPTER 10. THE BLINDFOLD

Candice felt nervous as she joined Olivia at her table at Andre's for a business lunch. It was cold outside but lovely and warm in Andres as she checked her long coat at the door.

Candice had not seen Olivia for some time and things between Aaron and her had been starting to return to normal.

Olivia was immaculately dressed in a black dress, silk stockings, and bright red lipstick. They kissed each other on both cheeks.

Candice had brought along the latest refinements of the new logo, letterhead, and web design for the rebrand for Olivia's company. Olivia looked through the designs with great interest complementing Aspire on their excellent work and attention to detail. They drank a substantial amount of red wine and enjoyed Andre's special of the day which was fresh lobsters with shellfish, vegetables, and herbs in bubbly, light vinaigrette.

After the talk about business was completed, Olivia produced a box wrapped in a red ribbon from under the table. Candice removed the ribbon and looked inside the box which contained bright red Victoria's Secret lingerie which was very lacy and sheer.

"A little present for doing such a fantastic job for me," Olivia smiled.

"I'm sure Charlie will love this," Candice joked, quickly closing the box before the other diners could see.

"Well, it's not for him. It's for you," Olivia said, "And I want you to try it on for me. Make sure it fits."

"Olivia, you are a very naughty lady," Candice whispered.

"So are you," Olivia whispered back, "Now collect your coat, go to the ladies room, change into the lingerie and leave the clothes you're wearing in the box. You can put the coat on over the top."

"You must be joking. What if someone sees me?" Candice whispered.

"No one will notice anything. Make it quick or I will change my mind about letting you wear the coat," Olivia whispered forcefully.

Candice frowned slightly and collected her coat as instructed from the waiter while Olivia enjoyed the last of the red wine before paying the bill.

Candice came out of the ladies room wearing her coat which was tan coloured, décolleté and went down to just above her knees. A slight hint of red bra could be seen above the top of the coat along with a delicious curve of cleavage. Candice wore black thigh-high tights on her legs. Olivia gave Candice a slight pat on the bottom as they exited the restaurant.

While walking to the car, Olivia playfully pulled at the coat, giving a passer-by in a business suit a flash of Candice's long legs.

Once they were in the car Olivia demanded to see the lingerie. Candice slightly opened the coat to show Olivia a flash of the red lingerie. As the interior of the car warmed, Candice was eventually coaxed into opening up the lower half of the coat.

Olivia used her hand to tap Candice's legs apart, firstly a small amount then a bit further.

"That colour really suits you. You are a hot, little minx who is always ready for sex," Olivia said, "Now I have a surprise for you but to get it you need to wear this."

Olivia dangled a black blindfold in front of Candice.

"What if I said no?" Candice said.

"Well that would spoil the surprise," Olivia said smiling and securing the blindfold over Candice's eyes.

No one outside the car seemed to notice Candice with her eyes blindfolded. The blindfold made her other senses acuter. Candice felt a tingle down her spine as Olivia started to stroke her between her legs over the red panties and caress the top of her thighs above the tights.

Candice could hear Olivia heart beat and how her breath slightly sped up. When they arrived at their destination, Candice heard Olivia say goodbye to the driver.

Olivia held her hand as she walked across what she assumed was the basement of Olivia's apartment building. In the lift going up, Olivia kissed Candice on the lips and flicked her tongue into Candice's mouth, swirling it around then kissed Candice along the neck with small kisses while stroking Candice's thigh and bottom.

Candice sensed another person was in the room as soon as she entered. She could hear two heartbeats, the gentle creak of another's footsteps and a muffled giggle.

The room was warm and gentle tango music could be heard in the background.

"Remove your coat, baby," Olivia whispered in Candice's ear, pulling the coat from Candice's shoulders, revealing her breasts clad in a red bra, her firm stomach, tight and shapely buttocks covered by the red lace of her panties, and her long legs clad in thigh high black stockings.

Olivia held Candice close and they danced together to the music, Olivia being careful to steer Candice away from any furniture. They danced slowly. Suddenly Candice felt another body dancing on the other side of her with them. The body was warm and soft, a woman's body.

"Hello, gorgeous. I'm Aurelia," the woman whispered in a husky voice into Candice's ear.

Candice turned to face the other woman and reached her hands out and brushed them against Aurelia's body, quickly realising she was naked.

"Go on explore Aurelia's body," Olivia encouraged Candice, holding Candice's hand to Aurelia's breast.

Candice stroked her hand against Aurelia's breast. It was firm and ripe like a peach with soft nipples. Candice gently rubbed her fingers over Aurelia's nipples causing them to slightly stiffen. Then Candice moved her hands over Aurelia's stomach and then legs which Aurelia parted slightly and guided one of Candice's hands to her vagina.

Candice was surprised how wet this woman was. Her fingers glided into Aurelia's vagina and Candice massaged the upper wall of Aurelia's vagina as Aurelia rocked forward with the movement of Candice's fingers.

"Pleased to meet you, gorgeous," purred Aurelia.

"Candice, sit down upon the sofa," said Olivia guiding her to the brown chesterfield sofa in Olivia's lounge room.

Olivia nodded to Aurelia who removed Candice's bra, freeing Candice's breasts. Her nipples were already hard and pointy. Olivia moved onto the sofa and knelt down and sucked on one nipple while Aurelia knelt down to suck Candice's other nipple from the other side while stroking Candice with long strokes along her body. The two women then jointly pulled down Candice's red panties, leaving Candice in her blindfold, thigh high black stockings and black high heeled shoes. They pulled Candice's legs wide apart so her sex was pink and exposed.

Olivia then knelt between Candice's legs and kissed her along the top of her thighs and then her inner thighs, brushing her hand in a gentle circular pattern over her sex.

Aurelia continued to kiss and suck each of Candice's nipples in turn then kissed Candice's mouth and neck.

Olivia then licked along the crease between Candice's legs until she came to her clit then gently licked and sucked Candice's clit.

Aurelia then put one leg on either side of Candice, who remained sitting on the sofa. Aurelia moved her torso forward to Candice's mouth. Sensing Aurelia's closeness, Candice reached out and brought Aurelia forward so that her mouth was in line with Aurelia's vagina so Candice could kiss Aurelia's belly, while holding Aurelia's firm buttocks with her hands, like eating a ripe peach.

Aurelia spread her legs a little more so Candice's hot tongue could flick into her vagina and stimulate her clit.

"You are a gorgeous woman and you have a gorgeous mouth," Aurelia moaned.

Olivia reached up and pinched Aurelia's bottom.

"Ouch," Aurelia said.

"Don't make me jealous," Olivia said before resuming her licking and sucking below.

When both Aurelia and Candice were on the verge of cumming Olivia decided that she wanted more attention.

"Hold on ladies," Olivia said, "I promised you both a surprise Aurelia get down off the sofa and open the top drawer of my writing desk."

Aurelia was reluctant to have Candice stop but knew there was no refusing Olivia. She walked over to the desk and opened the drawer and pulled out a thick black double ended dildo.

"Give it to me," Olivia demanded.

Aurelia walked over with a slight frown on her face and handed the object to Olivia.

"Candice, open your mouth," said Olivia as she edged the dildo slightly into Candice's mouth.

"Lick it, please Candice," Olivia commanded.

Candice gingerly licked the object, feeling all the build up of pleasure subside.

"Now suck it," Olivia requested.

Candice opened her mouth and had to strain to take the object in which Olivia moved back and forward.

"Keep your legs open," Olivia demanded as drool from Candice's mouth dripped onto Candice's vagina.

Olivia then slipped the dildo into Candice's vagina moving it back and forth and then put it in Candice's mouth again.

"OK now get down on the floor on your hands and knees please Candice," Olivia commanded.

Candice then got off the sofa and did as instructed. Her head resting down on the sofa.

Olivia then moved the dildo back into Candice's vagina from behind and moved it forwards and back and gently spanked Candice's bottom.

"Aurelia, could you please go on the other side," Olivia requested which resulted in Aurelia also going onto her hands and knees on the other side of the dildo so that her bottom was facing Candice's bottom.

Olivia also then gently spanked Aurelia's bottom.

"Never forget that I am always the most gorgeous woman in the room," Olivia chided then moved the other end of the dildo into Aurelia, moving it forwards and backwards to stimulate the two women.

"OK, now you keep that dildo moving. I don't want to see it stop until I am ready," Olivia said leaving the two women moving in time with each other, their bottoms facing each other as the dildo went deeper into their vaginas.

After Olivia had drunk a glass of wine she returned to find the women, red-faced and huffing.

"And remember don't orgasm until I say so," Olivia said swinging one leg over Candice's head then sitting astride it on the leather sofa.

"Candice, don't stop moving but you also have another job to do. You need to make me cum with your mouth," Olivia said, moving her vagina forward to Candice's waiting mouth.

Candice's tongue flicked deep into Olivia's vagina and licked along the sides and then forwards and backwards then sideways over Olivia's clitoris. Olivia reached her hands forwards and held Candice's head close to her crotch, moving her hips upwards so that Candice's tongue could penetrate deeper. Olivia luxuriated in the sight of the two beautiful young women having sex for her pleasure and the movement of Candice's tongue was so delicious within her that she felt sparks start to go off that then spread throughout her body.

"OK now remove the dildo and I want you to rub your vaginas together until you cum," Olivia requested.

Aurelia and Candice then interlocked their legs and rubbed their vaginas and breasts together until they were a hot panting mess.

Afterwards, Olivia, had both of the other women stand in front of her and she caressed each woman between the legs to find out which woman was most aroused. Not being able to decide she called the contest a tie.

CHAPTER 11. AARON'S CHALLENGE

Aaron worked hard to prevent a takeover of Harrison by Rosen Bank. Aaron had quickly gathered all the financial data about Rosen and found that they were in a very strong position to take over Harrison as they had an excess of capital and needed to expand to ensure further profit growth.

While researching Rosen Bank online he had discovered that Rosen also had a female CEO, Antoinette Ward, who had worked her way up from working as a teller, into middle management, senior management and then the Board of Directors. There was a photograph of a New York charity dinner online which showed Olivia together with Antoinette Ward with bright smiles clinking glasses together. Olivia had forbidden Aaron from talking to the other staff about the looming takeover. The only people who knew about it at Harrison were Olivia, Jill, and Aaron. Olivia had the information passed on to her by a senior stockbroker who had known her father.

While Aaron was still staring at the charity photograph online, Jill knocked on Aaron's workstation to get his attention.

"Aaron, you've been summoned," Jill said and turned in the direction of Olivia's office.

Aaron loved watching Jill walk. There was a beautiful swaying movement to her bottom under her tight houndstooth office dress. Jill had a slender neck under her brown bob. Aaron could detect a hint of a bra strap under her soft blouse. Jill had black glasses in a retro style that made her look like she had come from another era. Jill ushered Aaron into Olivia's office.

Olivia sat at her desk, flipping through a report that Aaron had prepared on resisting the takeover.

"Very good work, Aaron. But there is something missing from this report – on the ground intelligence," Olivia said.

"Yes, Rosen are keeping their cards very close to their chest," Aaron replied.

"That is why I have chosen you for a mission, a very important one. One that only you can perform," Olivia said running her hand over Aaron's chest.

"Yes. And what might that be exactly?" Aaron said, placing his hand on Olivia's hand to stop the movement of it.

"I want you to meet Antoinette, wine and dine her, and find out why she has singled out us for a takeover," Olivia said with a satisfied smirk on her face like she was settling some old score.

"Well that just sounds a bit improbable," Aaron said in reply.

"Not really. I have been doing my own research. Antoinette is on the books at a very exclusive dating agency which just happens to be run by an old friend of mine. Guess who is meeting her for lunch tomorrow?"

"Who?" replied Aaron.

"Peter Quirk."

"Who's he?"

"You," giggled Olivia.

CHAPTER 12. LUNCH AT ANDRE'S

Olivia had bought Aaron a new suit by Armani as well as new shoes and a blue silk tie. He looked like a male model who had just walked off the catwalk and attracted admiring glances from the surrounding tables at Andre's Restaurant. Olivia had profiled him as an investment banker so she thought she had to buy Aaron a suit to look the part. Aaron had changed into it at work as he did not want Candice to freak out when she saw the suit as she would have thought Aaron had cleared out their savings to buy it.

Antoinette turned out to be even more attractive in person than she was in the photograph Aaron had seen online. She was also charming and nice which made Aaron feel a creep for misleading her like this. Despite Aaron being much younger than Antoinette he found that they had a lot in common. They both loved baseball, enjoyed reading detective novels and both were Netflix addicts, enjoying many of the same serials. Eventually, the conversation turned to work and Aaron made up some stories about the life of an investment banker which Antoinette smiled and nodded to, perhaps she was just used to dates making things up to impress her.

Antoinette explained about the challenges she faced at work but was careful not to give up any company secrets and only obliquely referred to the takeover being planned for Harrison. Aaron tried getting Antoinette to talk about this further but Antoinette very politely changed the topic and got Aaron talking.

Aaron had two hours in Antoinette's company and it really flew by as far as Aaron was concerned. They agreed to meet again and Aaron gave Antoinette a number that Olivia had organised for him with a new telephone.

Aaron needed a drink after the lunch with Antoinette and stopped in at the strip club he had been to with Tom previously. He knew that Olivia would be anxiously awaiting the news of his spying but he wanted to make her wait and was also worried about having so little to offe despite her elaborate investment in the charade.

The waitresses at the strip club gave Aaron a lot of attention, at first thinking he was a high roller but soon lost interest after his meagre tips.

Aaron returned to work just before knock off time and was hoping that Olivia had already left. Unfortunately, for Aaron Olivia was still in her office, fuming at Aaron's delay.

"Get in here," Olivia demanded.

When Aaron entered he saw Jill sitting on one of the chairs at the desk, and she had a look on her face that said 'I can't believe this guy'. Notwithstanding all the trouble he was in, he could not help but admire Jill's legs.

"OK. Tell me everything you got. Jill will take notes," Olivia said.

"I'm sorry Olivia. There' really nothing to tell," Aaron said looking at the ground.

"Come on there can't be nothing," Olivia said.

"Nothing that is of any use to you, Olivia," Aaron did not look up.

"Look at you standing there," Olivia approached and poked Aaron in the chest, "What is the point of you? I don't get it. You're useless."

Aaron did not know what to say.

"That suit is worth more than you make in a month. Now get out of it. It's clearly wasted on you."

"What?" Aaron was incredulous. After all, he had done for Olivia. He could not understand why she was treating him like dirt.

"Strip. Do I have to spell it out for you?"

Jill turned away from Aaron as he removed his jacket and handed it to Olivia.

"And the pants," Olivia said pointing to them.

Aaron removed his shoes and then the expensive trousers. He also had expensive Calvin Klein underwear which also was bought by Olivia just in case things progressed with Antoinette as Olivia had hoped.

"Keep going," Olivia requested, enjoying the power she held over Aaron. She could make him do anything, she thought.

When Aaron was naked he stood covering his penis with his hands.

"May I be excused?" he queried.

"I'll answer a question with a question," Olivia replied.

"Who is the more attractive Jill or I?"

"You're both very attractive," Aaron muttered looking down.

"Jill and I were talking about you before. Talking about how good you would be in bed. She thought you might be all right but I know you would be lousy," Olivia adlibbed making Jill turn towards them and frown and shake her head.

"Are you going to tell me?" Olivia asked harshly.

"You are both very attractive," Aaron repeated.

"Well, that is what I told Jill you would say but that won't do. I made a little wager with my secretary Jill here and I want to collect. So you're going to have to tell the truth or we'll be here all night," Olivia said causing Jill to look at her watch. She was meant to be meeting her boyfriend in half an hour. Aaron was handsome though and obviously spent a lot of time in the gym with his chiselled features.

"I have an idea," Olivia continued, "Jill and I will take turns touching you and whoever gets the best reaction from your nether region will obviously be the most attractive."

Jill rolled her eyes but had got used to her bosses eccentricities. What Olivia did was scandalous but she was like Teflon, any trouble just seemed to wash off her back.

"Jill will start first," Olivia ushered Jill over with her hand.

Jill sauntered over on her high heels. Aaron's eyes met her eyes and they gave each other a smile.

"There we go," Olivia said noticing a slight upward lift in Aaron's penis.

Jill giggled and softly caressed Aaron's cheek with her hand.

"Nice skin," she said.

"OK, Jill. My turn now. Don't get carried away," Olivia said putting her palm on Aaron's forehead then moving it along his face, distorting his features, then moving a finger into his mouth.

Olivia looked down to Aaron's penis and was disappointed with the lack of action.

"You go again," Olivia motioned to Jill who moved her hand gently over Aaron's chest, gently brushing his nipple. Aaron's penis stirred again. Jill smiled at the success she had.

"I'd say the results are inconclusive. Let's try something else," Olivia said, "Take off your top Jill."

Jill seemed a little taken back by this request and for a moment, she thought about telling Olivia to stop her silly games and let her go to her date but despite all the silliness Jill liked working there and did not want to get on the wrong side of Olivia.

Jill unbuttoned each button of her blouse, revealing more and more of her cleavage until the blouse was removed. Aaron was now semi erect. Jill could not help but do a little clap in delight.

"Don't get too excited. My turn now," Olivia said, "Aaron go hold on to the end of my desk. That's it – so your bottom sticks out."

Olivia and Jill then discussed each detail of Aaron's naked anatomy and made comparisons of size in relation to other lovers while occasionally breaking into laughter. Aaron felt his cheeks redden with shame and with perverse pleasure. His erection though was unchanged from its previous position.

Olivia came in for a closer look, "I was right. He does find you more attractive. It is quite thick you know. I would like to see what Aaron here was capable of. You know what me winning the bet means don't you?"

"No, what does it mean?" Jill said.

"It means that you must do my bidding for the rest of the day," Olivia explained.

"I did not read that in the small print of the bet. I do have an appointment though with my boyfriend in twenty minutes and so all I can offer is fifteen minutes of doing your bidding and if you want me to do some typing then forget about it," Jill said cheekily.

"OK, then fifteen minutes will have to do. Now remove that sexy skirt of yours. I want to see you just in your underwear," Olivia said.

Jill removed her skirt and hung it over a chair and was about to remove her glasses when Olivia said, "No leave the glasses on. I want you to see what is coming next."

Jill looked over at Aaron whose penis was now standing almost painfully erect.

"Poor Aaron," Olivia said, "Need some attention?"

Aaron stopped looking at Jill's long legs clad in black stockings and returned to looking at the ground.

"Well, first you need to do something for Jill. I want you to peel those stockings off Jill and suck on Jill's toes. Are you capable of that?"

Aaron nodded. Matters had already gone too far to turn back. He looked into Jill's eyes and she smiled and gave him a peck on the cheek. He then peeled the stockings down Jill's legs then knelt upon the floor and took Jill's foot with both hands and started to kiss her toes one by one.

"I said suck on Jill's toes. Not kiss. Can't you get anything right?" Olivia criticised Aaron.

Aaron then took each of Jill's toes in turn and sucked them while massaging the underside of Jill's foot.

"Ah, those almost too intense," Jill said.

While Aaron was sucking on Jill's toes, Olivia ran her hand over Aaron's backside and back before landing a smack on one buttock.

"That is for being useless with Antoinette," Olivia said then she landed a smack on the other buttock and giggling, "And that is for having a very smackable bottom."

Jill joined in laughing then said, "Aaron, this has been ...well strange but I have to get going."

Jill quickly dressed then said, "I'll see you both tomorrow."

·

CHAPTER 13. DOMESTIC HARMONY

On the weekend Olivia asked Aurelia if she wanted to watch her favourite television show – 'Domestic Harmony' to which Aurelia replied:

"Sounds like drudgery."

"Just give it 5 minutes. You will see. I'm sure you will find it intriguing," Olivia said mysteriously as Aurelia wandered over to have a look.

"What is this?" Aurelia asked, "Some kind of reality TV show?"

"It's Candice," Olivia said.

"So it is," Aurelia said shocked the said "Olly, why do we have Candice on our TV?"

"Well, Aaron and I made a little arrangement. I would not make him pay me back for his Armani suit if he agreed to place a webcam in their bedroom for one weekend," Olivia said.

"You are wicked," Aurelia said, "Perhaps 'twisted' is more the appropriate word."

"Inventive," Olivia giggled.

"Mad," giggled Aurelia.

"Wait, look. Aaron has arrived in the room," Olivia said then got out her mobile and started typing.

Aurelia and Olivia then saw Aaron get out his telephone and read the message from Olivia. Aaron was wearing his new suit.

"The mouse takes the cheese," Olivia said.

"What are you up to?" Aurelia said.

"Just giving Aaron some helpful suggestions," Olivia said tapping on the screen of her mobile.

Aaron read his mobile. The text message said "Massage Candice's shoulders."

He put the telephone down by the bedside and started to massage his wife's shoulders, gently moving her long hair to one side. Candice was wearing a white satin nightie and Aaron moved the straps to the side so that the nightie dropped from her shoulders. He kissed Candice along the neck as he massaged her shoulders, smoothing away the stress of the day.

"That feels divine," Candice said turning and smiling at Aaron.

In Olivia's penthouse, Aurelia turned to Olivia and said: "Candice does have beautiful breasts."

"What would you like him to do to them?" Olivia smiled with a mischievous grin.

"Kiss around the areolae and then lick and suck the nipples," Aurelia said, satisfied with her choice.

Olivia got to work on her mobile, adding the instruction from Aurelia and then added her own instruction. *Then ask Candice to spread her legs wide and do the same thing to her clit.*

Aaron heard his mobile phone ping and subtly went to check it while still massaging Candice's shoulders with his other hand.

He slipped the mobile into the pocket of his trousers, removed his suit jacket and then knelt in front of Candice and kissed her breasts softly and then swirled his tongue around each nipple in turn and then sucked on each nipple in turn until he felt them harden.

"Candice, darling. Could you please spread your legs for me. Do it wide," Aaron could hardly meet the loving gaze from Candice, he felt he was falling.

Candice moved her legs apart on the end of the bed and Aaron started to kiss in a circle around her inner thighs then applied the flat of his tongue gently across Candice's clitoris before sucking on it gently.

Candice closed her eyes and then descended backwards onto the bed and moved her arm over her head to cover her eyes.

Meanwhile in Olivia's penthouse, the erotic display was starting to turn Olivia on and she placed a gentle kiss on Aurelia's lips.

Aurelia smiled and said, "Get Aaron to ask Candice to turn around and whip her with his silk tie and then take her from behind."

"Anything for you," Olivia replied and went back to her telephone and typed in the instruction.

Aaron heard his telephone chime in his pocket and sneaked a look at the screen while stroking Candice with his hand as she writhed on the bed.

"Candice, could you please turn over," Aaron said, removing his tie and unbuttoning his shirt. His chest was strong and muscular and his stomach rippled with abs.

Candice turned over so that she was face down on the bed with her legs on the floor.

Aaron pulled up her satin nightie away so that her bare bottom faced upwards, beautifully curved like a pale peach. Aaron ran his hands over Candice's bottom, admiring the soft warmth of her skin. He then picked up his silk tie from the floor and whipped it onto Candice's bottom. Candice turned around surprised but then smiled.

Olivia and Candice giggled with delight at the sight of it which was almost comical.

After Aaron had whipped Candice's bottom with the soft silk tie, he used his hands to move Candice's legs a bit further apart, so that he sex stared at him, hot and ready. Aaron then quickly unzipped his trousers, releasing a strong erection and gently eased himself into Candice. She swooned and arched her bottom upwards. Aaron then moved deeper and deeper into Candice.

Olivia turned her television off, "Let's leave them there. I want to recreate that all with you but first, can you go to your room and get dressed in that new black Agent Provocateur lingerie set I bought you. Also, can you put on those new black stilettos with the extra high heels?"

"With pleasure," Aurelia giggled.

•

CHAPTER 14. STORMY SKIES

The following day the clouds in New York hung low and dark grey burdened with rain about to fall. Everything in the city appeared to slow with the humidity.

Candice appeared to be out of sync with those around her, hurrying along the street in a red long coat and hat, in black stockings and high heels and carrying a small black box.

From time to time Candice checked her mobile to follow the route to the address that Olivia had given her which was in a part of the city that she had not been to before. Candice attracted sideways glances from men as she passed. As instructed by Olivia she had applied bright red lipstick to her lips and smoky eye makeup with false eyelashes. Candice was also wearing a long blond haired wig.

The address was down a narrow lane in the nightclub district of New York. The lane was empty apart from a large man in a black suit with a bald head and jet black sunglasses. Thunder rumbled distantly.

Candice nodded *hello* to him. If he nodded back it was imperceptible to her. He did not query Candice but opened the door to her. There were stairs at the entrance which descended into a lower floor. Candice could hear the slow throb of electronic music down below. She found it hard to adjust to the low red light in the club as she descended the stairs.

Candice was surprised to see elegantly dressed business women chatting with each other as they walked around the club or stood or sat around small stages or at the bar. A DJ with short spiky hair and black lipstick was at a booth on the side of one of the stages.

Candice felt disorientated for a short period before Olivia approached and hooked her arm around Candice's arm then placed a quick kiss upon Candice's cheek.

"You look fantastic, baby," Olivia said, "Come with me to the change rooms. They're at the back."

In the back room to the club women in various stages of undress huddled around lighted mirrors, applying makeup and straightening stockings.

"Ladies, this is Candy. It's her first time stripping so please help her out," Olivia said.

The women introduced themselves and welcomed Candice who nervously said hello and received their advice about what to do on stage.

Olivia had selected an outfit for Candice from the rack. It was a nurse's outfit with a dress that went only to half way down Candice's bottom and was secured with Velcro for easy removal. Olivia helped Candice put her wig hair up under a small nurse's hat and gave her some props which were a stethoscope and a small silver hammer.

Once Candice was dressed she watched the next strippers from the side of the main stage of the club. Olivia gave her a glass and a bottle of wine to calm her nerves. Candice drank the bottle quickly. She needed Dutch courage to get through this.

On stage, two beautiful French maids came on stage dressed in short black dresses, suspenders, and stockings with high heels. They stripped down to their lingerie and then caressed each other with feather dusters and wiggled their bottoms in front of the women in the front row. Some of the women were given the feather dusters to dust the maids' bottoms and elsewhere.

The next act was a young woman walking across the stage in a long dress, high heels, and jewellery. A second woman with short hair jumped on stage in a long coat and then flashed the first woman and they then simulated sex on the stage.

Candice became more and more nervous. Olivia then said, "It's your turn go."

Candice wobbled slightly as she left the sidelines and moved onto the stage.

"Give it up for Nurse Candy," the DJ announced over the PA followed by polite applause from the crowd.

At first, Candice was a little lost, blinded by the bright flashing lights in her face. She then started to sway from side to side in time with the throb of the electronic music, swinging her hips causing the short nurse's dress to rise up further revealing her lingerie clad bottom. Candice then turned around and bent over like the French maids had done and moved her bottom in time with the music. She then bent down and moved her hands up from her ankles up along her body then up into the air.

Not quite sure what to do next, Candice stepped down the steps at the front of the stage into the audience and asked one of the business women, "May I listen to your chest."

The woman laughed and nodded *yes*.

Candice leant down causing her breasts to spill out of the top of the nurse's dress and brought the stethoscope down onto the woman' blouse. This got a big round of applause from the audience and the business woman pinched Candice's bottom.

Candice pretended to listen to the woman's heartbeat and then said, "Very healthy and just a little bit naughty." This got another round of applause.

Candice then danced over to the next woman and stood with her legs standing astride the woman's legs and said, "Ma'am may I check your reflexes?"

"You sure can, sexy," the older business woman said.

Candice then tapped the silver hammer on the woman's leg and it lifted up between Candice's legs.

Candice mimed riding the woman's legs, swaying her arms from side to side.

The music then died down and the DJ said, "Put your hands together for Nurse Candy."

The audience clapped and whistled as Candice danced back to the change rooms.

"That was fantastic dancing Candy. I could tell the audience found it very hot. You are really talented," Olivia said as she cornered Candice in the change rooms, "Now have you got what I requested you bring?"

Candice nodded that she did and looked over to the small black box which was next to her clothes.

Olivia then leant in and whispered in Candice's ear, "Now I want you to take the box and go to the club toilets. Go into one of the cubicles but don't lock it. I'll be coming in there soon. Spread your legs and put the vibrator in and wait for me."

Candice's head throbbed from the wine and the constant throb of the electronic music. She picked up the black box and wandered in her nurse's costume down the hallway to the toilets. A few of the patrons said hello to her and congratulated her on her performance on the way. Candice just smiled and thanked them for the comments.

There were only three stalls in the toilets. Candice went into one of them and shut the door but did not lock it as instructed. She waited until the toilets were empty, sat on the toilet seat, spreading her legs and resting them on each side of the cubicle. Candice then took the small silver vibrator from the black box and moved it slowly into her vagina where it softly buzzed. Candice's heart was still racing from being on stage and all of the sensations made her feel light headed.

The door of the toilet swung open and there were the two business women from the audience that she had involved in her routine.

"Sorry sweetheart. The manager told us to come in here to see you. She said you wanted to meet us," the older woman said.

Candice crossed her legs, embarrassed by her wanton display.

Olivia then entered.

"So you have met Nurse Candy. I have to apologise for her. She finds dancing very arousing. Look it's very crowded in here. Why don't you all come back to my office? I have a full bar in there and some nice leather armchairs."

The business women agreed that would be nice and Candice followed behind them her head bowed, the vibrator clutched in her hand.

"Candy perhaps you could go sit in that chair over there. You can go back to what you were doing before. Don't mind us," Olivia grinned pouring the women and Candy glasses of champagne as they reclined into leather armchairs around Candice.

Candice sat with her legs slightly apart and half-heartedly stroked between her legs.

Olivia expressed her displeasure with a harsh glare and Candice spread her legs a bit wider. Olivia again looked displeased and Candice hung one leg over one armrest and one leg over the other armrest, giving the businesswomen an unrestrained view of her most private area.

Olivia nodded in the direction of the hand that held the vibrator and Candice switched it on and moved it into her vagina.

The business women studied Candice who had a look on her face which was hard to read. Olivia caught Candice's eye and she made the sign of a happy face across her own lips. Candice then started to smile.

"How's it feel, baby?" Olivia asked.

"Mmm," Candice replied.

"Are you wet?"

"Mmm," Candice replied.

"Would it be OK if one of these nice women felt you?" Olivia asked.

Candice felt like she had no choice but to nod. She pulled the vibrator out, leaving a small silver trail back to her vagina that glistened.

"Do I have a volunteer?" Olivia asked.

The older woman shyly raised her hand.

"We have a winner," Olivia announced.

The woman stepped forwards and traced her fingers along Candice's neck and the top of her chest then along Candice's legs and then gently brushed Candice's vagina with the knuckles of her hand.

"Definitely wet," the woman laughed.

The business women were not sure if this was real or just a show put on for them.

Whatever it was it was certainly hot, a welcome distraction from a long morning of meetings, telephone calls, and office gossip.

"Nurse Candy lie down over the top of the sofa," Olivia commanded.

Candice moved over the leather sofa so that her arms and legs dangled on either side of the sofa, the short nurse's dress framing her pert bottom.

The younger businesswoman then got up and ran her hands over Candice's legs and up to her bottom, massaging each buttock in turn then felt along the line between Candice's legs and massaged it gently.

"I suggest you use this," Olivia suggested picking the vibrator off the seat of the leather sofa and handing it to the woman whose cheeks were flushed now with a strong passion.

The woman looked for a moment on how to turn the vibrator on then it whirled into life. The woman brought it along the line between Candice's legs, massaging each soft crease with it then inserted it into Candice and pushed it deep into her so it was swallowed by her lips.

The older businesswoman was now at Candice's head, stroking her hair and neck then her face, gently stroking her cheek. Candice closed her eyes as the sensations built within her. It made no sense to her but she was entirely dominated by pleasure. It was a pleasure beyond reason. The older woman leant down and kissed Candice upon her lips. The kiss was so beautiful and gentle. The woman's scent was intoxicating and would remain with Candice for a long period of time as a sense memory.

The younger businesswoman and Olivia stroked her legs and bottom from behind while the older woman kissed her over and over again as the vibrator whirled. Candice then shivered with pleasure.

•

CHAPTER 15. THE HUNT

Olivia asked a select few to join her on a retreat at her mansion in the country to plan the fightback against the proposed takeover of her company. Jill, Aaron, and three other staff were selected to be part of the team working on the secret project. Olivia only selected those staff she knew she could trust or who were in her thrall. Aaron watched the large metal gates of the mansion close behind Olivia's car.

The mansion was high on the side of a mountain. It had once been a grand hotel but Olivia's father had decided to convert it into a country residence for the family. It had spa baths fed with naturally warm spring waters which were said to have health-giving properties. There was a large ballroom with high art nouveau arched ceilings. A small number of the mansion staff lived in cottages near the walls surrounding the property that once housed the staff from the hotel.

Aaron promised Candice that he would make it up to her and that he had no choice but to agree to have a planning meeting at his new work. He told Candice very little about his new job and had not disclosed that his new boss was a woman and especially not who she was. Aaron was equally unaware of the connection between Candice and his new boss.

Olivia, on the other hand, was aware of everything and derived great pleasure in the control and manipulation of others. She knew more about Aaron and Candice than they were prepared to admit to themselves. Olivia knew that they both reveled in being told what to do and the thrill of submission.

Olivia set up the war room in a large study that had been used by her father. In the morning, the team discussed each of Aaron's ideas for resisting the takeover of Olivia's company and in the afternoon developed detailed plans concerning putting each strategy into action.

Olivia asked Jill and Aaron to stay for dinner to discuss strategy further and arranged for the other staff to be driven home by her chauffeur. Aaron called Candice and wished her goodnight.

Olivia had organized for some of her friends to join them for dinner. The dinner was to be a masked dinner for fun. Aaron had been given a black mask and was advised to wear his Armani suit to dinner.

Olivia loaned Jill a sparkling long ball dress that Olivia had worn once for a Republican fundraiser. It had a low front and back with a long side split.

The dinner was held in a long dining room with wood-paneled walls lined with her father and grandfathers' hunting trophies, stag antlers and bearskin.

When Aaron entered the dining room all of the women turned to watch him. Aaron's muscles rippled under the sleek black suit. His thick black hair was slicked back and his olive skin glistened in the candle light. His dark eyes peered from his mask. Aaron looked over the seated diners and quickly realized they were all women. A waitress escorted him to his seat which was at the head of the table.

"Ladies of the Emporia Club, please welcome A to our dinner," Olivia said holding a glass of champagne aloft.

"To A," Jill proposed a toast, joined by the group of eight other women.

Aaron recognized Jill mainly by her voice. She had completely transformed in her appearance and looked more like a movie star than Olivia's secretary.

"Thank you, ladies," Aaron said as he took his seat.

"The menu today will be something very special ladies and gentleman," Olivia continued, "First up there will be an Arugula Salad with local figs, sherry vinaigrette, pine nuts, and manchego. Then there will be beef and chicken empanadas. To finish we will be going on a hunt in the grounds for our main course but I'll tell you more about that later."

The women chatted with each other excitedly. They appeared to be a variety of ages but from the beautiful dresses they wore, they all appeared to be from wealthy backgrounds thought Aaron. He chatted with the women either side of him who were exceedingly polite but gave absolutely nothing about themselves away, other than their interests in popular culture, the movies they had seen and their holiday destinations. Aaron soon realized that every member of the Emporia Club referred to other members of the club merely by an initial.

"What is the Emporia Club?" Aaron asked the dark haired woman to his left.

"We are just an organization that raises money for charity by holding dinners, events and the like. It's a social club for women with similar interests," the woman smiled looking deeply into Aaron's eyes.

"I was a member of Rotary for a period," Aaron said continuing the conversation.

The dark haired woman giggled and grabbed a bottle of red wine from the table and asked, "More wine?"

"Why not?" Aaron replied holding his glass out while his neighbor at the table poured.

"This is quite a treat. This is a 2009 Chateau Margaux Balthazar. Quite a rare and delicious drop," the woman laughed.

"I look forward to trying it," Aaron smiled.

"I look forward to trying you," the woman said laughing.

Aaron was not quite sure what the woman meant but laughed along.

After everyone at the table had finished their empanadas, the servants cleared the plates and left the dining room. Olivia then stood up and said, "And now for the main course we are going to all go on a hunt for a local delicacy. A delicious and tender meat - Aaron, please stand up."

Olivia had directed her voice and gestured towards Aaron who looked behind him.

"She means you," the dark-haired woman whispered to him.

Aaron shyly rose to his feet.

"This magnificent specimen has been hand reared and fed with only the best food, lean and muscular, and not an ounce of fat," Olivia joked and the women burst into laughter.

"Strip!" Olivia commanded. "But you can leave your mask on."

Aaron stood there a little bewildered.

The women then started to clap saying "strip" over and over again. Reluctantly Aaron undid his tie, removed his jacket and shirt. This was greeted with a round of applause by the Emporia Club.

"Keep going," one of the older women in the audience said loudly followed by laughter from the other women.

Aaron removed his shoes, socks and trousers so he stood before the women in his grey Calvin Klein trunks which bulged at the front.

"Don't stop now Aaron," said Olivia followed by more laughter.

Aaron then bent down and removed his trunks and covered his penis with his hands. He looked like a shy Chippendale dancer.

"Now let me announce the rules of the hunt. Rule number 1 - the prey will be given one minute to find a hiding place within the grounds before the hunt commences. Rule number 2 - the hunter who catches the main course will decide how we devour the main course and will have the first piece," Olivia said to more applause from the group as she walked over to the naked Aaron, slapped him on the bottom and said, "Off you go."

Aaron scooted off out of the dining room with his hands still over his penis.

"Congratulations Olivia. He has a very cute butt," one the women said to more laughter from the group.

Olivia then set off a timer on her watch and handed each of the women a lantern. When one minute had clicked over the women in their long ball gowns spilled out the door in search of Aaron.

Aaron had run straight for the gatehouse but found it unattended. Olivia had asked all the staff to return to their houses. The gate was locked and was too high to scale. He decided he would follow the fence

all of the way around in case there was another exit. While tracing th
fence he heard a small group of the women and saw their torche
swinging from their hands. The beams of the light from the torche
narrowly missed catching him. He crouched down behind a bush.

When they had moved away from him, he decided to retrace hi
steps the other way around. When he neared the gatehouse again he
heard dogs snarling and looked up the hill to see Olivia with two
Dobermans, straining against their leads.

Aaron double backed again but it appeared that the Dobermans had
picked up his scent. He could hear them still behind him. He ran along
the fence, his penis swinging from side to side unrestrained.

"Got you," a woman jumped out at him from one of the bushes and
wrapping her arms around him.

"I told you this would work," Olivia said, "The dogs are always the
best way to flush out the prey. Gets them disorientated."

The dogs now appeared quite docile as Olivia patted and scratched
them.

The woman who had caught Aaron held his hand as they walked
back to the dining room. Olivia produced a Chinese gong and hit it a
few times and all of the other women then returned to the dining room.

Aaron was not sure what was going to happen next. This was surely
the weirdest night he had ever had.

"Stand here Aaron," Olivia said and the women formed a semi-circle
of chairs around Aaron as he stood naked. He no longer covered his
penis with his hands. The women spoke quietly amongst themselves
about his size.

"The successful hunter tonight is Bernie," Olivia announced.

The women broke into applause again.

"Now Bernie will decide how we consume Aaron," Olivia
announced.

Bernice thought for a moment, then said: "First, let's tenderize him
by smacking that cute butt of his. Then let's have a nibble of that delicious

chest and fine sausage of his. And for the grand finale how about we give him a treat of mixed oysters."

The women laughed and clapped in approval.

"Turn around and bend forward Aaron," said Olivia to Aaron who was flushed with shame.

He turned around as instructed and presented his bare buttocks to the women for smacking.

The women formed an orderly cue and one by one rained down a smack on Aaron's buttocks with different levels of intensity. His bottom glowed red at the end of his spanking.

"Turn around Aaron," Olivia said, "And put your arms behind your head."

Aaron faced the women with his chest out and arms behind his head.

"Would you like some wine with your beefcake, madame?" Olivia said to the woman who had caught Aaron, in a mock French accent.

"Oui," the woman laughed in return and Olivia poured red wine over each of Aaron's nipples and his penis. The woman then leant down and licked each of his nipples and then licked his penis, which started to spring to life.

Olivia again poured wine over Aaron for the next woman and so on. At the end of all the female attention, his penis stood strongly erect. The women discussed his penis and made comparisons to their husbands, lovers and other "prey" they had enjoyed at the Emporia Club.

Once all the women had returned to their seats, Olivia said, "I'm sure you will all agree that A here has been a terrific prey tonight and as requested by Bernie there will be a reward for him. Aaron, could you please get down on the floor, on all fours. If you would like to give Aaron here a little reward then as he comes around I want you to pat him on his luscious hair, remove your panties and spread your legs. Ladies, I should commend him to you as being quite talented with his tongue."

Olivia grabbed Aaron by his hair as he crawled on all fours to the first woman, who happened to be the dark haired woman who was sitting next to him at the dining table. She stroked and patted Aaron's hair as if he was the favorite family pet. The woman then stood up and pulled her panties down and spread her legs wide. Aaron knew what was expected of him and licked the woman between the legs and sucked upon her clitoris. He enjoyed the woman's deep musky perfume. She continued to stroke his hair with one hand.

"That is so good," she moaned, completely shamelessly in front of the other women. They had been on many sexual adventures together so that almost nothing would shock them now.

The look of sheer pleasure on the dark haired woman's face made the other women so envious that not one of them rebuffed Aaron from getting *his reward.*

By the end of the evening, he was exhausted and ached with unfulfilled desire. He sat at the dining table and drank red wine as each of the women kissed him on the cheek as they went up to bed. At the end, only Olivia and Jill remained. Aaron could barely look either of them in the eye. Jill promised that she would take Aaron to an amazing restaurant the following day run by a husband and wife who made the best pies in America. Jill put her arm around Aaron.

"You do have an amazingly good technique for a man," Jill said in his ear.

"More red wine?" Olivia said to Jill.

"Just a drop," Jill replied with a mischievous grin.

Olivia again poured the wine over Aaron's chest so that it dripped upon the wooden table. Both Jill and Olivia then licked and sucked on Aaron's nipples which brought his erection back to life.

Jill then removed her ball dress and bra and swung her leg over Aaron and lowered herself onto his erection. Olivia studied him intently as he thrust into Jill with an almost savage passion, the result of so much frustrated desire. When Jill could tell he was about to cum she dismounted from him and sucked upon and stroked his penis until he exploded in a powerful orgasm which shot sperm onto the table.

Olivia looked at the panting Aaron and gave him a slow clap, kissed him on his cheek and walked to the door, hand in hand with Jill. Aaron watched Jill's naked bottom sway as she walked away from him. He wondered if he could ever tell Candice about all this.

CHAPTER 16. HOUSE OF GAMES

"Candice, it's that woman from Harrison on the line," Candice's secretary said after Candice had picked up her telephone. *What does she want now?*

"Hello, Olivia?" Candice said, looking out her window to the streets below.

"Hello, baby," Olivia said, "I've been thinking about you."

"I've been thinking about you too," whispered Candice.

"My driver is parked out the front of your building," Olivia said matter of factly.

"Yes?" Candice said, wanting to know what Olivia was up to.

"He's waiting for you," Olivia said.

"Yes, and why is he waiting for *me*?" Candice queried.

"So he can drive you to my country estate of course. I need to see you urgently," Olivia said.

"Can we not discuss the matter over the telephone?" Candice queried.

"I need to see you," Olivia said in a harsh whisper.

"OK, OK. I'll get my secretary to clear my diary," said Candice.

Candice quickly organized to clear any appointments in her diary, tried to call Aaron on his mobile but he was not answering and then caught the lift down to the ground floor where, as advised, Olivia's black limousine was parked right out the front, oblivious to the fact it was a 'no standing' zone. Perhaps the driver was also too intimidated or enthralled by Olivia to say 'no' to her.

The journey to the estate was beautiful. It was relaxing to get out of the city and see rivers, mountains, natural woodland, ferns, and birds. They arrived just after noon.

As they entered Olivia's estate the large metal entry gates opened and then closed behind them as they drove along the gravel road to the mansion. Everything about the mansion said 'old money'. Olivia came out to greet Candice when she arrived.

"I'm so glad you could come," Olivia said.

"Well, you did say it was urgent," Candice replied.

"It is. It is," Olivia said.

They walked into the mansion and Olivia showed Candice around and introduced her to the guests that she had staying with her who were all women, generally of a similar age to Olivia, one would have been a number of years older and one was younger than Candice, a beautiful young woman named Julie, who she felt most on the same wavelength with of all of the women at Olivia's estate.

Olivia had not explained the reason for the urgency of Candice attending the mansion when lunch was served in the grand dining room.

"Ladies of the Emporia Club. For our next meal we have two very special guests, Candy and Jules," Olivia announced to the gathered guests.

"A toast to Candy and Jules," one of the women said standing up and raising her glass. The others joined her in a toast.

"After lunch we are going to play some poker," Olivia announced and received a small round of applause.

The lunch was exquisite, made with mainly local produce and all cooked on site by Olivia's chef. One of the women explained to Candice that they just went by their initials for fun. It was a chance to escape themselves and their responsibilities in the real world where many of them held senior positions in business, the entertainment industry or politics.

After lunch, the women organized themselves into small groups to play poker.

"Are you going to play, Candy and Jules?" a dark haired woman said to Candice and Julie.

"No, I don't really know how to play," Candice laughed.

"Me neither," said Julie.

"It's easy. I'll teach you both," the woman said.

Candice and Julie watched a few hands and then summoned up the courage to play a hand herself.

"You're good at this," the woman commented to Candice and Julie after they had both won a few hands.

"Beginner's luck," Julie said laughing.

"I think we should make this a little more interesting," one of the other women said, "How about we play for money?"

"No, I don't think so," laughed Candice.

"Fifty dollars each. Each matchstick represents five dollars. What do you say?" the dark haired woman continued.

"Why not?" Candice said.

Julie nodded *yes* as well.

Both Julie and Candice's run of good hands continued and soon they both had big mounds of matchsticks next to them. They were having fun and Olivia's waiters kept on replenishing their wine glasses.

"How about we increase the stakes?" the dark haired woman said to the group.

"I'm listening," Julie laughed.

"Each matchstick is now worth fifty dollars," the woman said.

"Well I might just trade them in now," joked Candice.

"I haven't finished yet," said the dark haired woman, "The game continues until one of us hits the thousand dollar mark."

Candice tallied up her matchsticks and realized she was only fifty dollars or one matchstick short of winning overall.

"I'm in," Candice said.

"Me, too," said Julie.

"OK then. Let's play," the dark haired woman said.

The faces of the women around the table suddenly became impossible to read.

The woman next to Candice one the next round followed by a win by the dark haired woman. Olivia won a round of poker. All of the other women apart from Candice and Julie won the following rounds until both of them only had one matchstick left.

"Now, let's make this a bit more interesting," the dark haired woman said, "Let's make it the winner of the next round wins all the matchsticks and they are now worth one hundred dollars each."

"Yes?" said Candice.

"I'm interested," said Julie.

"There is a catch, however," the dark haired woman said, "You obviously only have one matchstick left and so something more needs to be added to the bet."

"Like?" asked Julie.

"A wish," the woman said smiling.

"What kind of wish?" Candice asked.

"Well, whatever the winner of the round wants. It has to be something within your power of course," the woman said.

Candice and Julie thought about the odds and did the rough calculations as to how much money in matchsticks there was.

"What the heck. I'm in," said Julie.

"Me too," chimed in Candice after a pause.

Olivia shuffled the cards and dealt them out.

The faces of the women around the room were inscrutable to Candice. Her hand appeared to be a winning one to her – four of a kind.

She played her hand followed by Julie who beat her with a straight flush.

The black haired woman then trumped them all with a Royal Flush. The woman tried hard at suppressing a smile. It twitched at the sides of her mouth.

"Sorry Candy and Jules, you now owe Bernie here a wish each," Olivia said.

Bernice thought for a moment then said, "I wish that Candy and Jules here would dress for us and put on a show for our entertainment."

"That doesn't sound so bad, does it, ladies?" Olivia continued, "I have some very nice clothes for you in one of the side rooms. You follow me and Bernie here."

Candice and Julie then followed Olivia and the dark haired woman as they walked across the wooden floor, down a corridor to a room with large mirrors surrounded by lights, there were a makeup table and a number of different costumes and dresses on racks.

"Let's go for Vogue style glamour with beautiful dresses and sexy stockings," the dark haired woman said getting some richly colored dresses from the racks, selecting matching black lingerie for Candice and Julie and then holding up stockings to the light to have a look at the patterns of the stockings.

Olivia then said, "Well don't be shy, show us how you look in these?"

Candice and Julie then stripped out of their clothes so that they were naked before Olivia and the dark haired woman.

"Hold on a sec, let me look at you," Bernice said, "Hey remove those hands from your body. Don't be shy. Both of you are gorgeous. You should be running down the streets naked and letting people enjoy your beauty."

For a moment, Olivia and the dark haired woman just stood and stared at the two beautiful naked young women before them.

"You know something. I think they would be even more beautiful if they were shaved," Olivia said.

"Their heads?" the dark haired woman expressed with mock surprise.

"No, their pussies," Olivia laughed, "Come on Candy and Jules with me to the bathroom."

When they got there, Olivia lathered up an old shaving brush and moved it up and down over Candice's pubic hair. The dark haired woman did the same thing with Julie.

"Spread your legs a little, baby," Olivia said to Candice who followed the direction she had been given.

Olivia then moved the brush backwards and forwards over Candice's vagina.

"This was my Dad's favorite shaving brush. I kept it as a memento of him. Good to put it to good use," Olivia said.

After applying the lather, Olivia produced a cut throat razor and sharpened it against a leather strap.

"This was also his. Now be still," Olivia said as she applied the blade to Candice's skin and shaved off a line of pubic hair then another until Candice was fully shaven. Olivia then shaved Julie in the same manner.

"Not bad," Olivia said, admiring her handy work then gave both Julie and Candice, a playful pat to their backsides.

Julie and Candice then returned to the dressing room and got into their expensive black lingerie, stockings and beautiful colorful dresses.

Before long they were on stage performing for the women as Aaron and Jill were approaching the mansion in an old green Stag sports car which had been loaned to them by Olivia so they could visit a local restaurant. Aaron had been trying to call Candice on her telephone without success.

Julie and Candice had their level of arousal judged with Julie being judged the clear winner.

"Now Candy, as the loser of this little competition, I award you the 'must try harder trophy'. Now come over to the entrance to this room," Olivia said waving Candice over and then said, "I want you to face away from this doorway and kneel with your head to the ground and your bottom up high."

Candice followed Olivia's instruction with her head low to the ground, so that her hair covered her face and her bottom was facing the doorway.

"Now snake that hand of yours between your legs and pull the lips of your pussy apart," Olivia continued.

Again Candice followed the instruction and held the lips of her vagina apart with two fingers from the same hand.

Just then Aaron walked in with Jill. Aaron was taken aback by the sight of the beautiful woman before him, displaying herself so wantonly. Notwithstanding a large number of women in the room watching him, he started to become aroused so that his penis pushed hard against the front of his trousers.

"Get it out again, Aaron. The ladies of the Emporia Club implore you," Olivia said as she came up to Aaron and stroked his chest.

Aaron unzipped his black trousers and pulled his penis out of his trousers. He stared at the woman before him and she seemed so familiar in the strange environment her found himself in. He studied the small freckles and other small marks on the back of the women as he stroked himself until his erection was strong.

The women in the audience clapped to show their appreciation of the size of the erection Aaron had achieved.

"She's waiting for you," Olivia purred.

Aaron leant over the woman and caressed her between the legs. She was so lubricated and aroused.

Aaron then brought his penis forward and entered Candice, who then turned to face Aaron.

Both of them were shocked as they recognized each other with Olivia reveling in the perversity of the moment.

"Go on," she whispered as they both were frozen mid-coitus as if they had looked upon the face of Medusa.

Olivia stroked the side of Aaron's cheek and then Candice's.

"Go on," Olivia encouraged them again.

Aaron then slowly again began to bring his penis forward into Candice, slowly building a rhythm. The women in the audience knew something was going on but they did not quite know what. They clapped along with the rhythm of the penetrations.

Candice was torn by so many different emotions and thoughts until her head was spinning, she closed her eyes and slowly the sensations in her body started to take over, until she was lost in the moment, and all he talking and clapping faded into the background and there was only the sound of their two heartbeats beating together.

•

Other books by the same author

The second book in the Erotica series is ***The Secretary: The Pleasure of Surrender***[1]. Jillian Allesbury will do anything to please her boss Olivia Harrison, surrendering to one sizzling sexual adventure after another from the boardroom to the bedroom.

Nicolas's novel, ***The French Maid***[2], tells the story of Zoé Fabrice, a beautiful Parisian student who obtains a vacation job at the chateau of the mysterious Martin Dore, an international businessman. He appears to live a life of complete material and sexual indulgence with a coterie of friends living the high life. Zoé is attracted to her employer, his life, and his friends but what lies beyond the glittering façade? *The French Maid* is the first book of the *Belle Fleur* series of books.

A short story in the series, *Leon and the Older Woman* is available upon subscription to Minuet Publishing.

---

1. *https://www.amazon.com/Secretary-Pleasure-Surrender-Erotica-Book-ebook/dp/ B01F0N33WS?ie=UTF8&ref_=asap_bc*

2. *http://www.amazon.com/French-Maid-Belle-Fleur-Book-ebook/dp/B01CUSGHTC/ ref=sr_1_1?s=digital-text&ie=UTF8&qid=1457737405&sr=1-1*

Subscribe to our mailing list

For a free story and information about new releases subscribe to: Minuet Publishing[3] at:

4

http://minuetpublishing.wix.com/books

Thanks for reading! Please add a short review where you purchased this book and let us know what you thought!

Don't miss out!

Visit the website below and you can sign up to receive emails whenever Nicolas Blanc publishes a new book. There's no charge and no obligation.

https://books2read.com/r/B-A-IHVC-TSDJ